To Ira, who always lives life to the fullest
—Margaree King Mitchell

To the memory of James "Pie" Harris
—JER

Pecan Flats is a fictional town based on Hickory Flat, Mississippi, close to where the author was raised.

Amistad is an imprint of HarperCollins Publishers.

Text copyright © 2012 by Margaree King Mitchell
Illustrations copyright © 2012 by James E. Ransome

Manufactured in China.

Library of Congress Cataloging-in-Publication Data
Mitchell, Margaree King.
When Grandmama sings / by Margaree King Mitchell ; illustrated by James E. Ransome.—1st ed.
p.   cm.
Summary: An eight-year-old girl accompanies her grandmother on a singing tour of the segregated South, both of
them knowing that Grandmama's songs have the power to bring people together.
ISBN 978-0-688-17563-4 (trade bdg.) — ISBN 978-0-688-17564-1 (lib. bdg.)
[1. Segregation—Fiction.   2. Grandmothers—Fiction.   3. Singing—Fiction.   4. African Americans—
Fiction.   5. Southern States—History—1951—Fiction.]   I. Ransome, James, ill.   II. Title.
PZ7.M6937Gs   2012   2008034353   [E]—dc22   CIP   AC

Typography by Rachel Zegar
12   13   14   15   16   SCP   10   9   8   7   6   5   4   3   2   1
❖
First Edition

When Grandmama Sings

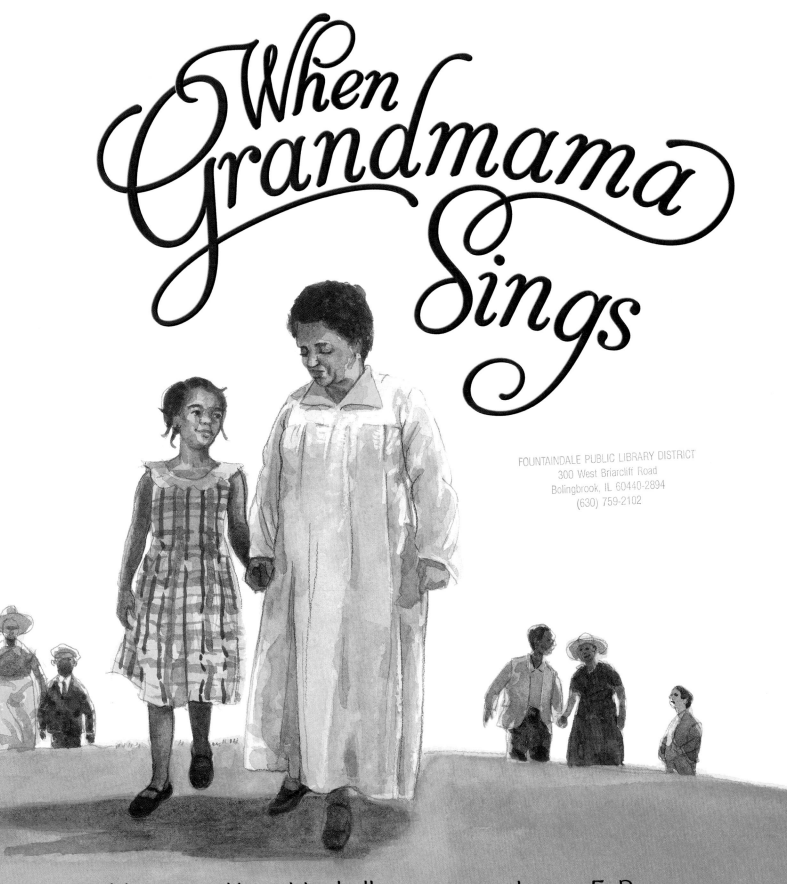

By Margaree King Mitchell   Illustrated by James E. Ransome

Amistad
An Imprint of HarperCollinsPublishers

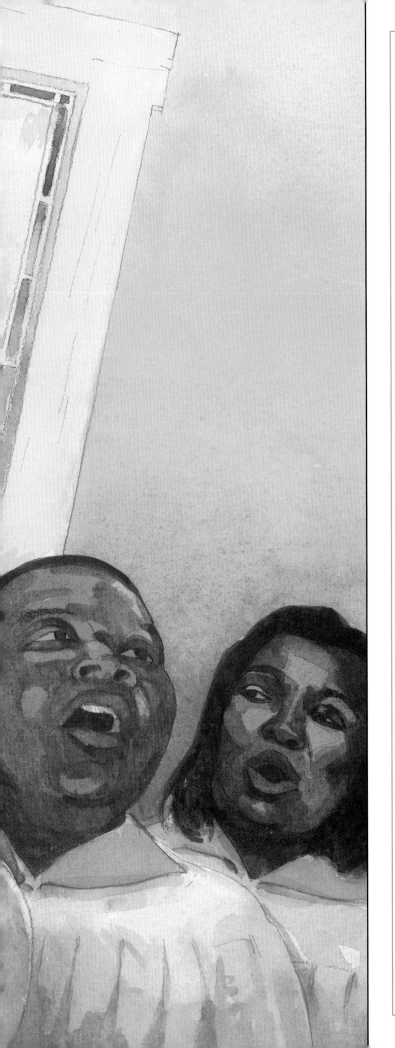

My Grandmama Ivory Belle Coles loved to sing. She sang in the church choir. She sang while she cooked and cleaned and worked in the garden. Whenever she wasn't singing, she was humming.

We lived in Pecan Flats, Mississippi. The summer I was eight, Grandmama would come by the house and listen to me read to my sister, Carrie. Grandmama couldn't read herself. But she always had a song to sing.

People in Pecan Flats loved to hear Grandmama sing.
Whenever there was any kind of party, they always asked her
to sing a few songs. After my cousin Roby's wedding, one of
the guests, Mr. Reynolds, asked Grandmama if she had ever
thought of singing outside Pecan Flats. Grandmama had
wanted to, but she'd never had the chance. Mr. Reynolds offered
to book her and a band on a small singing tour of the South.

When Grandmama told us she was going to accept Mr. Reynolds's offer, I begged her to take me with her. "I've never gone anywhere either," I said. "And I can help you read signs and menus and such."

Daddy shook his head. "I don't like the idea of you being so far from home. You know how hard things can be for colored people out on their own."

Mama looked at Daddy. "Belle won't be alone. She'll be with family, and she can help out her grandmother. She'll be all right."

Grandmama pulled me close. "I want Belle to go. She will be a big help to me."

That settled it. I was going on tour with Grandmama.

The day before we left, Mama and Daddy had the whole family over for a good-bye dinner. Aunt Mattie and Uncle Sam brought a sweet potato pie for dessert. After dinner, Grandmama sang a song. My favorite part was:

I sing because I'm happy,
I sing because I'm free,
For his eye is on the sparrow,
And I know he watches me.

Grandmama knew everything was going to be all right. That made me feel good.

Uncle Sam gave me his lucky rabbit's foot to take on our trip. He hugged me good-bye. "You be safe and look after your grandmama, hear?"

The next morning three big old cars drove up to our house. I wanted to ride in the car with the instruments, but Grandmama asked me to sit up with her in the lead car.

We traveled on two-lane paved highways that took us through many small towns that looked like Pecan Flats.

Out in the countryside we passed farms, mule barns, small churches, and abandoned buildings. Grandmama was nervous but excited too. So was I. But the soothing hum of her voice comforted me.

In Biloxi, Mississippi, Grandmama was booked to sing in a high school. I sat in the front row and read while Grandmama and the band rehearsed. But I couldn't keep my mind on my book because her singing was so powerful. The way she clung to each note captivated me.

That night only seventeen people showed up. I was so disappointed for Grandmama. Then the band began to play and I heard Grandmama's voice soaring through the auditorium. It sounded as if she was singing to a room full of people.

I saw the folks nodding and smiling as Grandmama sang:

> *"One of these mornings*
> *You're gonna rise up singing*
> *You're gonna spread your wings*
> *And take to the sky . . ."*

I felt like she was singing directly to me.

Afterward we drove through town. We passed restaurants and hotels, but we didn't stop. I pointed out the "WHITES ONLY" signs to Grandmama. Everything was segregated just like in Pecan Flats. Even famous black entertainers had to stay in hotels that were just for black people. So when we got to our hotel, we saw Ella Fitzgerald. Grandmama and Mr. Reynolds were excited that we were all staying in the same hotel.

We spent the next day on the road to New Orleans. We didn't even stop to eat. When we got to the club, the manager told Grandmama he wasn't going to pay us.

The band didn't want to play for free. I felt sad for Grandmama. But she took me by the hand and headed backstage. "I'm singing with or without music," she said.

The band decided to play and followed us backstage. It was a good thing they did. A man who booked acts for a big theater in Atlanta was in the audience. He booked Grandmama and the band for a performance after the tour.

The show ended at midnight, and we drove around looking for food. The only place open had a "WHITES ONLY" sign on the door. Before anybody could stop her, Grandmama pushed the door open and took me inside.

"I can't serve you," the waitress told Grandmama.

"Ma'am, I've got a hungry granddaughter and a band outside, and none of us have eaten all day," Grandmama replied. She put some bills on the counter. "You know what's right," she said. "Do what's right."

We went back outside. I was so hungry, my stomach ached. I held tightly to my rabbit's foot.

When all the customers had left, the waitress came out and handed Grandmama a brown paper sack. We eagerly bit into baloney sandwiches. I was glad I didn't have to go to bed with an empty stomach.

The next week Grandmama and the band had shows in Texas and Arkansas. In Little Rock Mr. Reynolds found a story in the newspaper about Grandmama's performances in Texas. I read it to Grandmama. We were so excited. Folks were starting to write and talk about Grandmama's singing.

In Alabama the police stopped us just as we entered Mobile. We had to get out of the cars and explain who we were, where we were

going, and why. We stood on the side of the road while the police
went through our bags and dumped everything on the roadside.
I didn't know what they were looking for, and they didn't say. I held
Uncle Sam's rabbit's foot tightly in my hand.

After they left, we picked up our things and dusted them off.

"Welcome to Alabama," Mr. Reynolds said softly.

We finished the tour in Alabama without any more trouble. Atlanta, Georgia, would be Grandmama's last show. The Magnolia Theatre was the biggest one I'd ever seen. It was a real theater, a whole block long. To me it looked like a palace.

Grandmama was singing for an audience of white and black people. The white people sat on the main floor while the black people sat in the balcony. It made me sad. It was just like home and everywhere else: people kept apart from one another.

But for a while Grandmama's voice lifted them all out of their seats and brought everyone together. When it was over, the white people were calling for more just as loud as the black people. It was a happy noise, and we all sounded the same.

It was a great night for Grandmama and the band. After the show I rushed back to Grandmama's dressing room and gave her a big hug. She smiled at me, but her eyes were sad. "Belle, tonight was special. I could feel all of those folks with me. I want us to feel this way all the time. I want to sing in a place where black people and white people aren't kept apart," she said. "That's the kind of world I want for you."

When we got home, I had so much to tell Mama, Daddy, and Carrie about the places we had been and the things I had seen. And how Grandmama's songs had the power to bring people together.

A few days later, Grandmama came by with a telegram. I read it to her. It was an offer from a record company up north, where things were a little easier for black people. Grandmama wanted to go.

We said good-bye to Grandmama and Mr. Reynolds at the train station in Memphis. I knew Mr. Reynolds would take care of Grandmama and help her with reading.

I was so proud of her. She'd never stopped singing her songs regardless of the size of the audience. She always knew things would work out. Now her music would go around the world. The promise of her song helped me believe in myself.

As she got on the train, Grandmama turned to me and said, "Someday you'll sing your own song, Belle."

And I knew I would.